MW01103574

My Family, My Home

Book Two

by Dawn Skinner

Illustrated by Matthew M. West.

ROTTEN

FOXY

SPYKE

JOSH

GRANDMA
ERICKA

SHARON

GOOD-
BUDDY
JOHN

GRANDPA
GEORGE

DOCTOR
DAX

BOULDER

LUCY-BLU

PIPER

BRYANNA

DORA

CHEF
PIERRE

WINTON

INTRODUCTION

This is a once-upon-a-time series of stories that take place when the world was very different from what it is today. A time when the simple things in life really mattered.

Turn the page and embark on a journey of discovery through the lives of these charmingly flawed characters. Love, laugh, and maybe even shed a tear with them as you discover your favorite dysfunctional friend.

Opening the bedroom door, Foxy looked around the room. Her best friend, Sharon the Shrink, had helped her for the past month to make the bedroom just right. They had shopped for gifts, new clothes, and the perfect boy's bed. Rotten and Spyke had painted the walls. Everything was ready.

I hope he likes it, she thought to herself.

"Josh will think this bedroom is great," Foxy heard her husband, Rotten, saying. "It's time to go. He will be waiting for us."

Foxy sat fidgeting as they drove to the orphanage. "Foxy, you will make a great mom to Josh," Rotten said, smiling at her.

Foxy smiled back.

She was excited to be adopting a child. She had enjoyed raising her stepson, Spyke, but he was almost grown up, and she knew she still wanted to make a home for another child.

Anxiously waiting outside of the orphanage, holding his suitcase, eleven-year-old Josh could hardly wait for Rotten and Foxy to pick him up. This would be a day he would never forget. He would be part of a family — something he had never known. From the moment he had first seen Foxy, he knew he belonged with her. She would be the mom he had never had.

Rotten's truck was slowly pulling up. He saw Foxy in it, waving at him. With a big smile, he waved back and ran to the truck. Foxy jumped out and gave Josh a big hug.

"I am so excited!" Josh said. "Are you sure you really want me?" he asked, with a bit of fear in his voice.

In a warm voice, Foxy said to Josh, "Of course we do. You are our family and our boy now. We have a bright future ahead of us."

"This is the best day of my life!" Josh said as he looked at Foxy and put his suitcase in the truck.

Rotten and Foxy smiled at one another. "Let's get you to your new home!" Rotten said. Josh didn't look back as they drove away. That life was behind him and he was starting a new one.

"Should I call you Foxy or Mom?" Josh asked.

"What would you like to call me?" Foxy answered.

He hesitated, thinking about it. "I want it to be special. I'll think about it for a while," he said.

"Can I call you Papa Rotten? Is that OK?" Josh asked Rotten.

"Of course you can," said Rotten.

As they drove along, Josh looked out the window. It was so beautiful this time of year. The leaves on the trees were changing color. Down the hill and around the bend, he saw a sign that read, "Welcome to Hamtown. A Good Place to Live!"

Driving down Bacon Strip Avenue, the busiest street in town, he watched with wide eyes. Josh couldn't believe he would finally live in a town. He looked in amazement at how busy it was. Rotten honked the horn and waved to the older man sitting on a bench. The older man waved back.

"That's my father, Grandpa George. He's the grandpa of everyone's heart," Foxy explained to Josh. "He sits there every day on his bench just watching everyone. You will meet him later."

Pulling up to their house, Josh saw a big sign that read, "WELCOME HOME, JOSH!" He laughed with excitement.

Rotten's teenage son, Spyke, came running out of the house. "Hi, Josh!" he said, as he tousled Josh's hair in a way that said he was happy to meet him. "We're brothers now."

"I've never had a big brother," Josh confessed.

"You have one now. Come on. I'll show you your room," Spyke said, grabbing Josh's suitcase. "That's my bedroom," he said, as he pointed. "Your bedroom is right next to mine," he said, and showed Josh to his room.

Josh stepped inside his bedroom. He quietly looked around.

"I hope you like it. I tried to think of what you might like, but we can change it to exactly what you want," Foxy said as she entered the bedroom.

"Change it? Never! It's great! I've never had my own bedroom. We all shared one big room at the orphanage," he said in a voice full of wonder.

Looking at the clothes on the bed, he said quietly, "I've never had new clothes. Someone always wore them before me. Thank you, Foxy. You got me a train set, too! I've always wanted one."

"One day, I hope you will travel and see the world by train," Foxy said.

"Come on! I'll show you the rest of the house," said Spyke as they left the room.

Josh stopped to look at all the pictures on one of the walls in the hallway. "Foxy calls this her 'wall of memories,'" Spyke explained. Josh looked at them with wonder on his face. He saw that the pictures told the story of this family's life through the years. "Your picture will be up there, too. You just wait and see," Spyke said. "After all, this is your family and your home now."

They continued looking at the pictures together, Spyke explaining each one.

In the kitchen, Foxy was busy preparing food. Family and friends would soon be coming to meet Josh.

Foxy heard the front door open. She could hear Rotten's mom, Grandma Ericka, saying to someone outside: "Come on, boys! Just carry it in here. Move that couch out of the way and put it right there."

Foxy hurried to the living room to see what was happening. She saw Rotten's friend Good-Buddy John, the best-looking man in town, and Spyke's teenage friend, Boulder, carrying in a piano. Grandma Ericka was dressed in an elaborate, flowing opera dress. Her makeup was gaudy and overdone. She always pretended to be someone else.

Oh, brother! Get a grip! Foxy thought to herself. *I wonder who she thinks she is today? One thing is for sure: she's crazy.*

"Grandma Ericka, what are they doing?" Foxy asked, hiding her irritation.

"Sometimes, Foxy, I wonder if you can even see out of those eyes of yours. Do I have to explain to you what these boys are doing?" replied Grandma Ericka in a scolding voice.

Continuing to scold Foxy, Grandma Ericka said, rudely, "How many times do I have to tell you I'm not Grandma Ericka?" Trying not to let her temper get the better of her, Foxy held back her words.

"I'm Olivia-Sophia!" Grandma Ericka said with an air of importance.

Ignoring Grandma Ericka, Foxy said, "Close the door before a mouse gets in here. That's the last thing I need in my house."

Rotten helped Good-Buddy John and Boulder put the piano where Grandma Ericka ordered. Everyone always did exactly what she wanted and no one dared to stop her.

Spyke and Josh came quickly to see what all the commotion was about. Spyke began to laugh under his breath when he saw Grandma Ericka. He loved her crazy personality. She always made him laugh. He could never figure out why Foxy would get upset with her instead of seeing the humor in it all. He leaned over and whispered to Josh, "That's my Grandma Ericka. She's a little crazy but she sure can bake a pie! All the kids love her."

"This is Josh," Foxy said proudly as she introduced Josh to Good-Buddy John and Boulder. "This is Grandma Ericka, Rotten's mom," Foxy explained to him.

Ignoring Foxy, Grandma Ericka said, "I've been waiting to meet you, Josh. As usual, Foxy never remembers who I am. I'm Olivia-Sophia, the famous opera singer. I'll be performing a song just for you today. This piano is my gift to you."

"Thank you! I don't know how to play the piano. No one has ever gotten me anything like this!" Josh exclaimed, as he looked at the piano in awe, pressing a few keys.

Grandma Ericka continued. "I believe every child should learn to play a musical instrument. Music is a wonderful part of life and I want you to learn it well. I will come every week to teach you."

Foxy couldn't believe what she was hearing. *Grandma Ericka would be coming every week!* Quietly, Foxy opened the front door and stepped outside, gently closing the door behind her. She let out a high-pitched scream that could be heard across town.

Grandpa George and the beautiful teenager Bryanna were on their way to Foxy's house. "Did you hear that scream?" he said with a laugh. "That's my girl, Foxy. Grandma Ericka must be at her house. We better hurry up. I think my Foxy needs me."

Foxy took a deep breath. *I feel so much better now. It's amazing what a scream will do for you!*

Family and friends soon arrived to welcome Josh to his new family and home. Lucy-Blu came with her guitar to sing a song or two. Bryanna and Spyke seemed in a world of their own as they talked together. Spyke teased her, Bryanna giggling at his playful way. Josh noticed how much they liked each other. They looked so cool, like they belonged together.

Josh interrupted their conversation. "You like each other, don't you? Bryanna is really pretty, isn't she, Spyke? Are you going to marry her one day?"

Bryanna and Spyke looked at one another bashfully and turned red.

They were relieved to hear Grandma Ericka order everyone to crowd around the piano and quiet down. She announced, "I'm going to perform a song for everyone." She sat down, straightened her opera dress, closed her eyes, and began playing. Everyone's attention was on her. She played very well. She broke out singing in an opera voice. Every note was perfect. No one had ever heard Grandma Ericka sing like that before, not even Rotten. He watched in amazement. Foxy stood, dumbfounded, listening to her. *How could this dysfunctional, frustrating woman sing like that?* She was full of surprises. Everyone applauded when she was finished. She stood up and took a bow, enjoying all the attention.

Someone knocked at the door. It was Sharon the Shrink, Foxy's best friend. "Is Josh here?" she asked Foxy, excitedly.

Foxy introduced Josh to Sharon. Sharon asked Josh how he liked his new home. While she was talking, her eye caught Good-Buddy John coming toward her.

"Hello, Sharon," he said in his deep, masculine voice.

All of a sudden she began to stutter, "Hello G…G…Good-Bu…Buddy John."

Why does this always happen to me when I see him? she wondered to herself. Her face turned red from embarrassment. Her nervousness got the better of her and, instead of stuttering, she began to laugh. As she laughed, she began to snort.

Good-Buddy John, always so innocent, thought he had missed something funny, so he laughed along with her. Josh couldn't figure out either one of them, so he hurried off to be with the teenagers.

Sharon quickly excused herself from Good-Buddy John, tripping over her feet as she made her way to the kitchen to help Foxy put the food on the table.

As Good-Buddy John watched her, he thought to himself: *Her feet and her mouth don't work too well. I've never met anyone who stumbles and stutters as much as her.*

It was time to eat. Josh looked at all the food on the table. He put a tiny bit on his plate.

Quietly, Foxy said to him, "Take as much food as you like, Josh, and don't be shy."

"I'm not shy, Foxy. The orphanage didn't like it if we took too much food," he whispered to her.

"This is your home now. There will always be enough food for you," she reassured him.

Josh smiled at her and loaded his plate up.

They ate, sang songs, and played games.

The day had gone by so fast. It was time for everyone to say goodbye.

As Josh lay in his bed that night, he could hear Spyke in his bedroom listening to music. Foxy and Rotten were in the kitchen talking in low tones. Even though it was very quiet, it all seemed so loud to Josh. He was used to absolute silence at the orphanage when it was lights out. He tossed and turned, trying to fall asleep.

Foxy quietly opened Josh's door to check on him. He pretended to be sleeping. She quietly closed the door. He smiled, feeling safe knowing that she would make sure he was asleep. He thought he heard the sound of a mouse scurrying across the floor. He put his pillow over his head to drown out the noises and fell fast asleep.

The next morning, he woke to the sound of Foxy making breakfast. He jumped out of bed, excited to begin another day. Foxy was stirring a mixture in a big bowl. She looked up to see Josh smiling at her. "Good morning, Josh."

"Good morning!" he said, as he yawned and stretched. "Whatcha making?" he asked.

"Waffles. I hope you like them!"

"I've never had waffles. Where's Papa Rotten?" Josh asked.

"He's gone to work at the Piggy's Pantry," she replied. "Could you put the plates on the table for me, please?"

Foxy continued stirring the waffle batter. All of a sudden, she saw a mouse run across the floor on the other side of the room and under the hutch. Foxy screamed, "A MOUSE!!" and, dropping the bowl of waffle batter on the floor, quickly jumped on a chair, shaking in fear.

Josh jumped up on the chair with Foxy and screamed with her. Spyke came running out of his bedroom. He almost began to laugh out loud seeing Foxy and Josh standing on the chair, screaming. At the same time, Spyke felt bad for Foxy, knowing how terrified she was of mice. "Are you scared of mice, too?" he yelled at Josh above Foxy's screams.

"NO!" Josh yelled.

"Why are you screaming then?" Spyke asked with a confused look.

"I felt sorry for Foxy, so I thought I would keep her company," he yelled back.

"Get rid of the mouse! It's under the hutch!" Foxy demanded, almost in tears.

Spyke quickly grabbed the broom and moved it along the floor under the hutch. The mouse scurried out, running all over the kitchen, Spyke chasing it with the broom. "Josh, get off the chair and open the door so it will run outside!" Spyke said, excitedly.

As Josh quickly flung the door open, there stood Glütten, the biggest lady in town, holding her gift for Josh. She had been about to knock on the door. The mouse, in terror for its life, ran toward the open door, and ran straight up Glütten's leg. Glütten began making little jumps, shouting, "Ouch, ouch," while trying to hit the mouse that was hiding under her clothes and running all over her. Throwing the gift to Josh, she began screaming and running away down the street as fast as she could with that little mouse inside her clothes trying to find its way out.

Spyke and Josh stood in the doorway, laughing until their sides hurt and tears ran down their faces.

"That's probably the most exercise Glütten has gotten in her life," Spyke said, between his laughs.

"That poor mouse probably died of fright!" Josh exclaimed, as they continued laughing.

Even Foxy joined in laughing when she got control of herself.

They went to Piggy's Pancake House for breakfast and spent the day showing Josh the town.

Josh would soon start school in Hamtown. Life would be so different for him here.

At night in bed, Josh again had trouble falling asleep. It seemed so loud when Spyke played his music and Foxy and Rotten talked in low tones. He again pretended to be asleep when Foxy opened the door to his bedroom to check on him. He put his pillow over his head and fell fast asleep.

SCHOOL BEGINS

The morning arrived for his first day of school. Foxy took a picture of him. Starting school in Hamtown was exciting and a bit scary. Josh had never really liked school. Foxy reassured him that school would be easier as he made new friends and got used to all the changes.

"Your first day of school is just one day and then . . . it's over. After your first day you will feel better," Foxy said, as she walked with him to school.

"I hope the kids like me," he said.

"Josh, if someone doesn't like you, then they are the ones that will miss out not knowing you," Foxy reassured him, then added, "You're a great kid. You're kind and good. I'm so proud of you!"

Three young boys were playing together in the schoolyard. "Hi, Foxy!" they called out as they came running toward her.

"Hi, Oliver, Ryan, and Little-Boy Ethan!" Foxy said. "This is Josh. Would you show him around the school?"

"OK! Come on, Josh!" Oliver said, as the four of them hurried off together.

Foxy watched with a smile on her face. She knew Josh would fit right in.

Josh got through that first day and Foxy was right. *The first day is only one day*. He knew he could do this again and maybe even like school.

That day, Foxy hung the picture she took of Josh on her wall of memories.

The next day in the schoolyard, the boys played catch together. A big, strong older boy came walking toward them.

"Come on! Let's get out of here!" Oliver said, in a panic.

The boys ran to the other side of the school.

"Who was that guy?" Josh asked.

"That's Tusk, the meanest boy in school. He likes to punch the younger boys and says mean things to them," Oliver explained.

"He calls me 'Four-Eyes' and makes me feel really bad about myself. Some days I don't even want to come to school," said Little-Boy Ethan.

"His parents and his big brother, Taylor, are really mean, too," said Ryan.

"That's why he's so mean. He's just doing the only thing he knows how to do. He probably doesn't like himself, so he doesn't like anyone else," Josh said.

At noontime, the boys all sat on the steps of the school eating their lunch together.

Tusk snuck up on them. "Look at all the losers eating their lunch!" he said, in a sarcastic voice.

Little-Boy Ethan felt scared and sick to his stomach.

"Hi, I'm Josh. Would you like some of my sandwich?" Josh asked him.

"Who do you think you are . . . Mr. Nice Guy?" Tusk taunted.

"I just thought you might be hungry," Josh replied.

"I'm not hungry!" Tusk yelled. "You're the new pretty boy, aren't you? You like being a pretty boy, don't you?" Tusk taunted, trying to insult and intimidate Josh.

"No, I don't mind being a pretty boy," Josh replied, making light of the situation. "I can't help how I look. I was born that way. I'll probably grow up to be really handsome. Are you sure you don't want a sandwich?" he asked, and reached out to offer Tusk half of his.

Tusk just stood there, unsure of himself. No one had ever tried to be nice or share anything with him. Usually, kids just ran away. He laughed at the idea that Josh thought he would be handsome one day. "I am a little hungry." He took the sandwich and walked away eating it.

The boys looked at Josh in awe.

"Weren't you scared?" Little-Boy Ethan asked.

"Yeah," Josh replied, as he let out a big sigh of relief. "Tusk is insecure. He feels like he doesn't belong. I realized that his insecurity was bigger than my fear of him."

A few days passed. Josh didn't mind going to school. He liked being with his new friends.

Tusk didn't bother the younger boys when Josh was with them.

One afternoon as the boys were throwing the ball to each other, Tusk came running toward them. Oliver threw the ball to Josh. Tusk ran right in front, catching the ball. "Look at the pretty boy, playing catch with all the losers!" he said, as he threw the ball hard at Josh, trying to hit him with it.

Josh quickly moved, dodging the ball.

Tusk laughed, mocking Josh. The teacher was coming over to see what was happening. Tusk quickly ran away. As he passed by Josh, he snarled, "I'll get you next time, pretty boy."

After school that day, Josh waited for his friends. Tusk ran toward him. "I told you I would get you later, pretty boy!" He punched Josh in the eye and kicked him in the stomach.

It happened so fast. Josh fell to the ground, not saying a word.

Tusk laughed in his face and, turning to go, said with a snarl, "It's your own fault. You deserved a punch on that pretty face of yours."

Josh slowly walked home. His stomach hurt. His eye was burning from the pain.

"What happened?" Foxy exclaimed.

"I'm OK, Foxy," Josh replied.

"Did that bully, Tusk, punch you?" she asked, all upset, as she cleaned up his eye.

Josh didn't answer.

"It's OK to tell me, Josh. Don't keep it to yourself," Foxy said.

"Wow! That's a shiner!" Spyke said, as he looked at Josh's eye.

"It's nothing. I got lots of black eyes at the orphanage," Josh said, trying to shrug it off.

"I got a few of those when I was your age, from that bully, Taylor. Did his brother, Tusk, do this to you?" Spyke asked.

"Yeah," Josh said, slowly.

In a frustrated voice, Foxy said, "That whole family is mean! How dare he punch my boy!"

"Calm down, Foxy," Rotten said. "Tusk feels like he doesn't belong. What goes around comes around. One day, someone will do the same thing to him. If this happens again, I will make sure it stops."

Josh walked to school the next day thinking about how he could avoid Tusk. Tusk didn't come to school that day. Josh felt so relieved. Walking home after school, he could see three boys fighting. One of them was on the ground being kicked. Josh slowed down, looking for another way home. The two boys ran away. The boy on the ground wasn't moving. As Josh came closer, he could hear him moaning in pain. It was Tusk.

He got what he deserves, Josh thought to himself. . . . But then he realized Tusk needed help. He was bleeding. *Should I help him or just leave him?* Josh was struggling to make a choice. In his mind, he heard Rotten's words: *Tusk feels like he doesn't belong.* He saw Bryanna and Spyke and how they belonged together. He saw himself and how he belonged with Foxy and the family he now had.

"I can't move!" Tusk groaned.

"I'll get help! I'll get the doctor!" Josh said, hurrying as fast as he could. He soon returned with Dr. Dax to take care of Tusk.

"Thanks, Josh," he heard Tusk say as Winton the ambulance driver and Dr. Dax lifted him into the ambulance.

Josh knew he had done the right thing. Tusk would get better in time. Would he appreciate what Josh had done to help him? Only time would tell. For now, Josh could feel good about himself, knowing he didn't treat Tusk badly.

As the days passed, Josh began to fit into his life in Hamtown, and his black eye slowly healed.

One evening as a warm breeze was blowing, Josh and the family went for a walk down by the lake. Josh walked next to Foxy, talking about many things.

"Tusk just wants to belong somewhere or with someone, right? We all want that, don't we?" Josh asked Foxy.

"Yes, Josh. No matter who we are, we want be seen and heard and know we mean something to others," Foxy replied.

As they walked along quietly, Josh looked up at Foxy and said, "I've decided what I want to call you."

"You have?" Foxy asked.

"Yes. I want to call you Mom," he said.

"I thought you wanted to call me something special," Foxy said.

"That's why I want to call you Mom, because Mom *is* special. There is no other word that means more to me when I think of you," Josh said, as he looked at Foxy with a look full of love.

Foxy couldn't speak as her eyes filled with tears. She just reached out to touch him softly as they walked along.

That night as Josh lay in his bed, he heard Spyke listening to music in his room and Foxy and Rotten talking in low tones in the kitchen. It wasn't loud at all, he thought to himself. He could hear Foxy quietly opening his bedroom door to check on him. He pretended to be asleep. She quietly closed the door. This time, he didn't put his pillow over his head to drown out the noise.

As he drifted off to sleep, he felt very safe. He thought to himself, *Sometimes, you know where you belong. Yes, this really is MY FAMILY AND MY HOME.*

ANNA

BABY
EASTON

BABY
EDEN

GLÜTTEN

BILL-
WILLIAM

KATY-
KATHERINE

LITTLE-BOY
ETHAN

LITTLE-
GIRL LEXA

ELLIE

AMAREENA

OLIVER

RYAN

HERMAN

LADY
EVELYN

MELANIE

TUSK

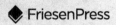 FriesenPress

Suite 300 - 990 Fort St
Victoria, BC, V8V 3K2
Canada

www.friesenpress.com

Copyright © 2016 by Dawn Skinner
First Edition — 2016

Copyright to Ageless Stories Inc.

All rights reserved.

No part of this publication may be reproduced in any form, or by any means, electronic or mechanical, including photocopying, recording, or any information browsing, storage, or retrieval system, without permission in writing from FriesenPress.

ISBN
978-1-4602-7347-0 (Paperback)
978-1-4602-7348-7 (eBook)

1. JUVENILE FICTION, FAMILY, ADOPTION

Distributed to the trade by The Ingram Book Company

CPSIA information can be obtained
at www.ICGtesting.com
Printed in the USA
LVOW05s2155141016

508758LV00006B/15/P

9 781460 273470